CASA BLANCA

OCT 2 9 2002

RIVERSIDE PUBLIC LIBRARY CBL

P9-CJY-531

Copyright © 2000 by Nord-Süd Verlag AG, Gossau Zürich, Switzerland.
First published in Switzerland under the title *Freunde*.
English translation copyright © 2000 by North-South Books Inc.

All rights reserved.
No part of this book may be reproduced or utilized in any form
or by any means, electronic or mechanical, including photocopying,
recording, or any information storage and retrieval system,
without permission in writing from the publisher.

First published in the United States, Great Britain, Canada,
Australia, and New Zealand in 2000 by North-South Books,
an imprint of Nord-Süd Verlag AG, Gossau Zürich, Switzerland.

Distributed in the United States by North-South Books Inc., New York.

Library of Congress Cataloging-in-Publication Data is available.
A CIP catalogue record for this book is available from The British Library.
ISBN 0-7358-1150-4 (trade binding)
1 3 5 7 9 TB 10 8 6 4 2
ISBN 0-7358-1151-2 (library binding)
1 3 5 7 9 LB 10 8 6 4 2
Printed in Belgium

For more information about our books,
and the authors and artists who create them,
visit our web site: www.northsouth.com

Pirkko Vainio
The Best of
Friends

Translated by J. Alison James

NORTH-SOUTH BOOKS
NEW YORK · LONDON

Hare sat and stared at his reflection in the lake.
The wind rippled the surface of the water, changing
the way he looked from moment to moment. It made
Hare wonder about himself.

Next to some animals, Hare thought, I am big and strong.

But compared to most animals, I am just a little hare,
nothing special. It made Hare feel so small.

One day a big brown bear called out to him.
"Hello, little Hare! Want to play?"
At first Hare was afraid. The bear was really
a very big animal.

But the bear bent down and smiled at Hare.
Then she swooped him up on her shoulders. Hare
had never seen the world from such a height!
Then they sat together, talking and laughing.

They played all afternoon, and by evening they were the best of friends.

When it was dinnertime, Bear caught them a fish.
But Hare didn't care for fish, so he brought them some
carrots. Bear liked the carrots a lot.

That night, Hare told his whole family about his
new friend Bear. They all wanted to come and meet her.
They stayed up telling stories until long after dark.
At last they all fell asleep snuggled in Bear's warm fur.

From then on, Hare and Bear played together
whenever they could. When danger was in the wind,
Hare just hopped on Bear's back, and away they flew.

When snow fell and the days grew short, Hare
helped Bear find a cave to sleep in. And whenever
Hare grew lonely, he'd venture out to find his friend.
Hare was warm and his sleep was deep when he was
nestled in Bear's paws.

In the early spring, Bear woke up. Hare leaped
for joy. He bounded up the mountain, calling to
Bear to join him.

The mountain was tall, and Bear was still tired.
Hare couldn't carry Bear, but he could wait
patiently and call out encouragement.

When they reached the top of the mountain, Hare said, "I'm so glad you finally woke up. I missed you."

Bear smiled. "Well, I'm here now," she said. "And we'll have lots of fun again."

Then they sat together and watched the sun go down—little Hare and big Bear, the best of friends.